Note to Reader:

There are numerous stories in Jewish lore about Elijah the Prophet disguised as a poor or elderly traveler appearing to worthy individuals, bringing blessing or good news. It is a cherished belief that he will herald the good news of the Ultimate Redemption and the coming of the Messiah. The illustration of the mysterious guest in this book is not meant to be a portrait of the prophet's exact features, but the artist's idea of one possible disguise.

Much, Much Better

To my parents, who raised their children in a home filled with blessings. C.K.
For Jamie and Bill with love. J.S.

First Edition - Elul 5766 / September 2006

Softcover Edition - Sivan 5768 / July 2008

Copyright © 2006 by HACHAI PUBLISHING
ALL RIGHTS RESERVED

Editor: D.L. Rosenfeld
Managing Editor: Yossi Leverton
Layout: Eli Chaikin

ISBN: 978-1-929628-43-8 (Softcover Edition)
ISBN: 978-1-929628-22-3 (Hardcover Edition)
LCCN: 2005938544

HACHAI PUBLISHING
Brooklyn, New York
Tel: 718-633-0100 Fax: 718-633-0103
www.hachai.com info@hachai.com

Printed in China

Adapted from Stories of Elijah the Prophet by Yisroel Y. Klapholtz, vol. 4, p. 159. Mishor Publishing, 1990.

Glossary:

Kiddush ..... Blessing recited over a cup of
wine on the Sabbath and Jewish holidays

Shabbat .... Sabbath

Torah .... The Five Books of Moses;
the law and wisdom contained
in the Jewish Scripture and Oral Tradition.

*You will notice the term "G-d." There are
some who will not write the full name in print,
wishing to avoid the chance that the written
word can be erased or thrown away. The belief
is that the name is holy, must be treated as
such, and reserved for ritual use.*

Much,
Much Better

by Chaim Kosofsky
illustrated
by Jessica Schiffman

Long ago in the city of Baghdad, Shlomo and his wife, Miriam, lived in a bright, tidy house. They were thankful to G-d for what they had, and shared with others when they could.

Every Friday, Shlomo straightened the books and swept the floor. Miriam spread a spotless white tablecloth and set the table.

"Three china plates and three crystal glasses, three forks, three knives, and three spoons for Shabbat," she'd say.

"I wonder who will be our guest this week."

Shlomo would smile at his wife.
"We'll have to wait and see. Shabbat
wouldn't be the same without a guest."

But one Friday night, when Shlomo came home, his eyes were sad and his face downcast.

"This has never happened before," he said to his wife. "Every traveler, every lonely or poor person, already had a place to eat. We have no guest for Shabbat."

"Don't give up so easily, Shlomo," said Miriam. "If we truly want a Shabbat guest, why don't we go and look for one?"

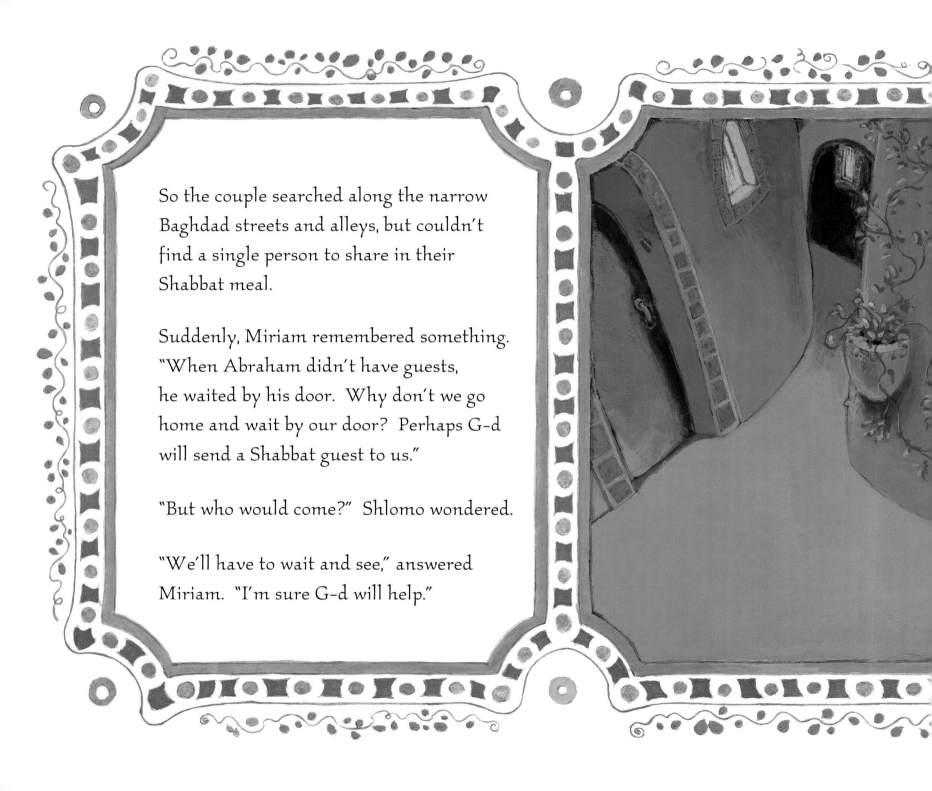

So the couple searched along the narrow Baghdad streets and alleys, but couldn't find a single person to share in their Shabbat meal.

Suddenly, Miriam remembered something. "When Abraham didn't have guests, he waited by his door. Why don't we go home and wait by our door? Perhaps G-d will send a Shabbat guest to us."

"But who would come?" Shlomo wondered.

"We'll have to wait and see," answered Miriam. "I'm sure G-d will help."

Back home, Shlomo opened the door. He and Miriam stood looking out into the darkness – waiting and listening. Then, moments later, along came an old man they had never seen before.

"I don't know anyone in town," he said sadly. "I have nowhere to eat the Shabbat meal."

"Please come in," said Shlomo. "My wife and I did not want to eat without a guest!"

What a perfect evening! After Kiddush, they washed their hands and ate the fresh, crusty loaves. There were stories and songs, and words of Torah. They ended by thanking G-d for the delicious meal.

When dinner was done and the candles burned low, the old man got up to leave. "I will always be grateful for your kindness," he said. "May G-d bless you and make your home much, much better."

"What do you mean?" asked Shlomo, glancing around at the comfortable room, the beautiful table. "What could be better?" The guest thought for a moment. "It would be better with a sticky, stained tablecloth."

"Better?" asked Miriam.

"Yes," said the guest. "And it would be much better with your books out of place."

"Much better?" Shlomo frowned.

"Absolutely," said the guest. "And it would be much, much better with crumbs scattered on the floor."

"Much, much better?" repeated the surprised couple.

What strange things to say! They walked their guest to the door and stared after him as he disappeared into the night.

"What kind of blessing is that?" asked Miriam. "What did he mean?"

"I can't imagine," answered Shlomo. "We'll have to wait and see!"

Many months later, when the mysterious guest was long forgotten, Miriam gave birth to a baby boy. The new parents were delighted. They named their son Yitzchak.

Yitzchak was a lively baby. He liked to wave his arms and legs, and he soon learned to roll over by himself.

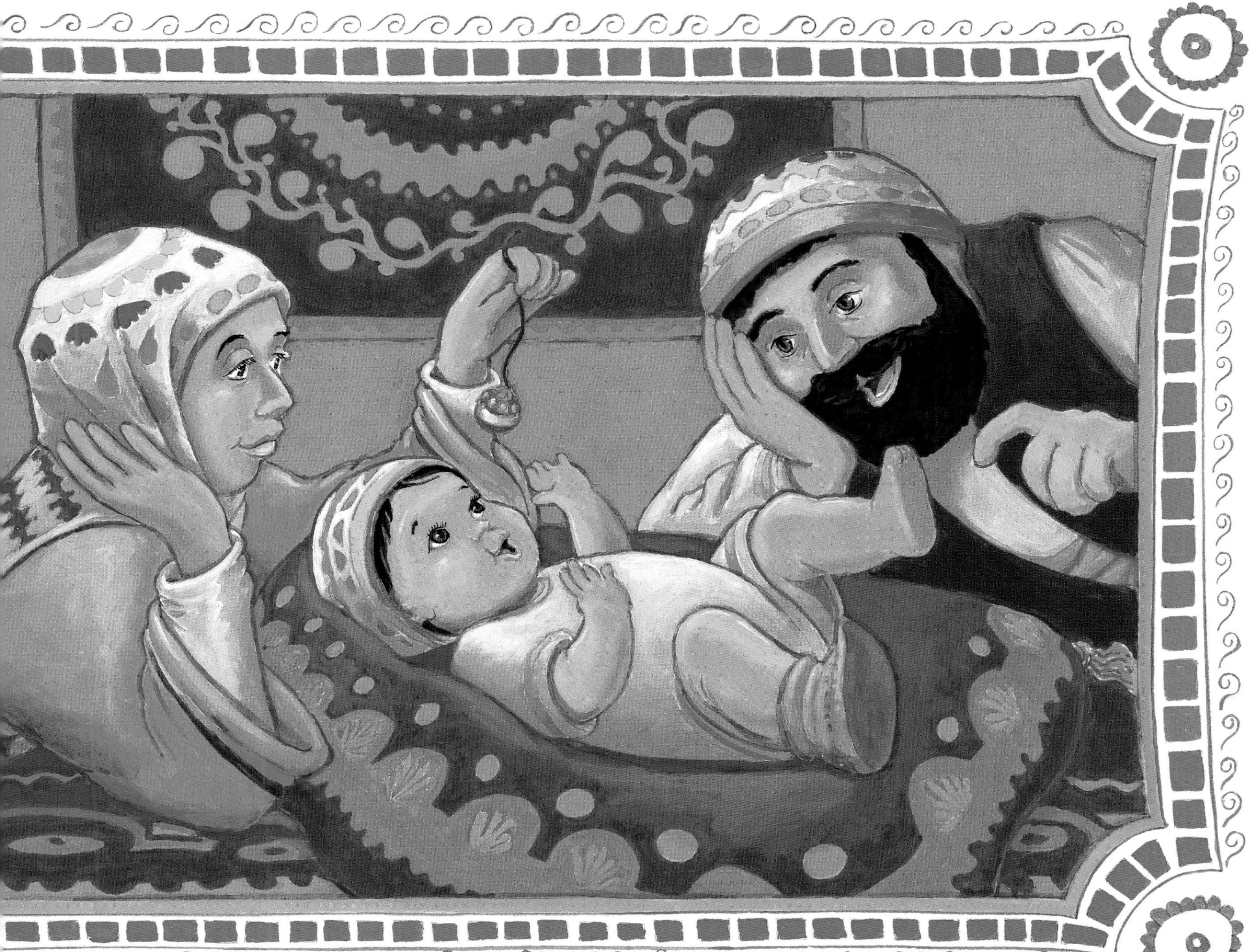

One Friday, while Shlomo and Miriam got ready for Shabbat, little Yitzchak was trying to crawl. He reached out with his arms and pulled himself forward. He could do it!

Slowly, Yitzchak crawled to the Shabbat table, grabbed the tablecloth in his little fist, and pulled. Over went the Kiddush cup! A sticky puddle spread across the table.

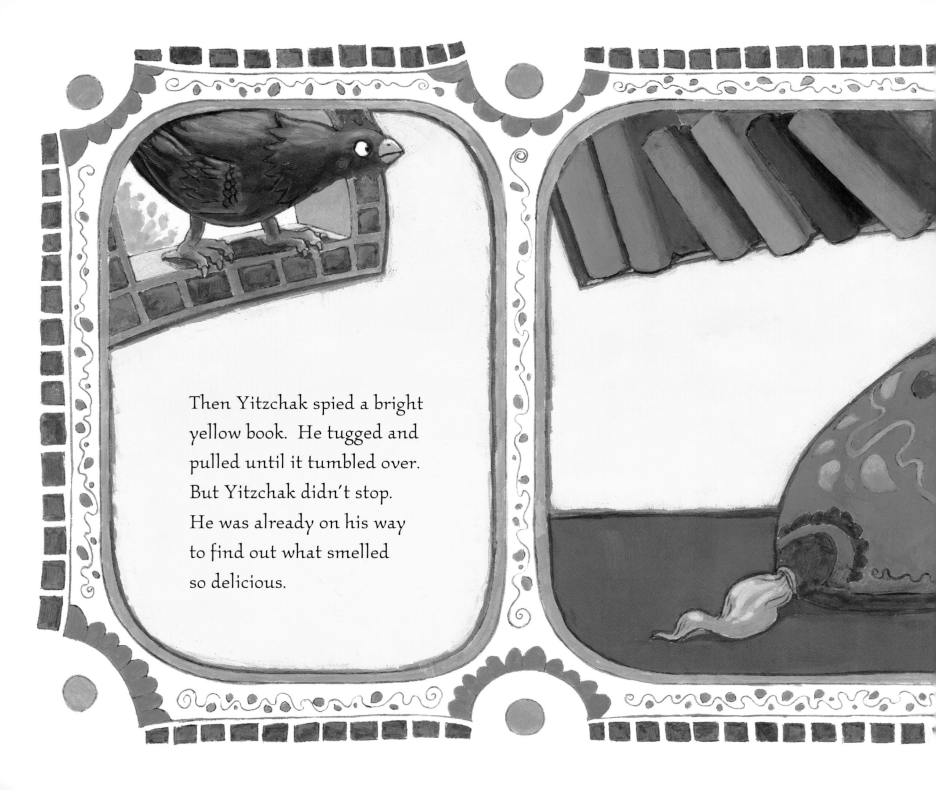

Then Yitzchak spied a bright
yellow book. He tugged and
pulled until it tumbled over.
But Yitzchak didn't stop.
He was already on his way
to find out what smelled
so delicious.

Yitzchak followed his nose to the wonderful smell. Crumbs fell here and there as he nibbled the soft, warm bread.

Just then came a knock at the door.
Standing there was the same old man who
had been their guest before.

"Please come in," said Shlomo. "You're just in time
to join us for Shabbat once again."

The guest stepped inside and
smiled as he looked around
the room.

Shlomo and Miriam looked
around, too. What do you think
they saw?

The tablecloth was sticky and
stained, the books were
out of place, and crumbs lay
scattered on the floor!

"Well," Shlomo said to their guest,
"your words have certainly come true!"

Miriam nodded happily. "Our baby is the best blessing in the world. Now our home *is* much, much better."

The old man bent down and picked up the precious little boy.

"He will welcome guests of his own one day – just you wait and see!"

The End